shaggydoggs®

SORROW FINDS JOY!

A new term starts at Apple Trees.
Headmistress Hoot waits by the front gate.

To meet and greet the birds and the bees.
No one wants to be last or late.

The bees make a beeline for the blossom.
To play hide and seek among the buds and flowers.

Sorrow sits on a branch all sad and lonesome.
All feathers and feet, Sorrow cries and cowers.

The bluetits and the blackbirds play five-a-side.
Between old apple cores to score.

Sorrow wants to be on the wing out wide.
Painful new shoes, Sorrow's feet are too sore.

6

Four funky pigeons coo and call out the latest song.
Rapping and clapping to the foot-tapping beat.

Sorrow clicks and clacks along.
Off-key, Sorrow stops this talon-curling tweet.

A couple of crows nest for a birds-eye view.
Telling tales of flying further afield.

Sorrow has stories to tell too.
Scared to speak, Sorrow's beak is sealed.

Seven starlings prepare for the school show.
Humming, strumming, drumming, and making a din.

A round of robins models the modern styles.
Bright red jumpers and fancy logos.

Sorrow looks on and smiles.
Black and white, Sorrow knows that little goes.

14

Two turtle doves recite poetry.
Rhyming words of peace and love.

Sorrow recalls friends and family.
Homesick, Sorrow scours the sky above.

A pair of woodpeckers play chess.
Making moves at a rapid rate.

Sorrow follows more or less.
Knight takes King, Sorrow sees checkmate.

Headmistress Hoot sounds the first lesson.
To count and record but no Joy to discover.

Then in bounds Joy full of jolly expression.
Perching beside, Sorrow finds Joy - a friend forever.

Sorrow has lunch with Joy up high.
On cloud nine with happy eyes.

Sorrow hands Joy a juicy maggot pie.
Known simply as *magpies!*

One for Sorrow.
Two for Joy!

One for Sorrow,
Two for Joy,
Three for a girl,
Four for a boy,
Five for silver,
Six for gold,
Seven for a secret,
Never to be told,
Eight for a wish,
Nine for a kiss,
Ten for a bird
You must not miss.

PICTURE BOOK CLUB

GAVIN THOMSON

SONIA J   17,18

OLIVIA J   5,6

EMILY R   SORROW + JOY

SAESHA P   1,2

IRIS S   19,20

DAISY A   3,4

ALARA M   7,8

SERAPHINA W   9,10

LANI S   13,14

ANNABEL G   5,8

AMBER D   5,6

BEATRICE P   3,4

AMINA F   5,6

SIYONA P   1,2

OLIVIA M   11,12

ANKIE B   21,22

SOPHIE M   11,12

KSENIA S   19,20

ROXANA F   1,2

MILLIE G   15,16

SOFIA B   15,16

SADIE G   3,4

MOLLY C   23,24

SANA B   13,14

FREYA S   7,8

SORROW FINDS JOY!

Printed in Poland
by Amazon Fulfillment
Poland Sp. z o.o., Wrocław